FOR AMY

Copyright © 2011 Pranas T. Naujokaitis

Balloon Toons® is a registered

trademark of Harriet Ziefert, Inc.

All rights reserved/CIP data is available.

Published in the United States 2012 by

🍎 Blue Apple Books

515 Valley Street, Maplewood, NJ 07040

www.blueapplebooks.com

Printed in China 07/12

HC ISBN: 978-1-60905-099-3

2 4 6 8 10 9 7 5 3

PB ISBN: 978-1-60905-183-9

2 4 6 8 10 9 7 5 3 1

BALLOON TOONS®

The TOTALLY AWESOME EPIC QUEST of the BRAVE BOY KNIGHT

by Pranas T. Naujokaitis

colors by Amy Rumbarger

BLUE APPLE

THE EPIC QUEST BEGINS

CAN YOU SET THE TABLE FOR BREAKFAST, HONEY?

NO WAY! SETTING THE TABLE IS BORING! BOY KNIGHTS DON'T SET TABLES!

VROOOOM

EXCUSE ME, YOUNG MAN?

SORRY, MOM...

NOVEMBER

GOLLY! WHAT A RELIEF!

THANKS! I'VE BEEN TRYING TO GET THAT CAR OUT FOR **WEEKS!** IT WAS MAKING ME SUPER CRANKY!

NO PROBLEM.

KNIGHTS ON PATROL

WE HAVE TO PATROL THE KINGDOM.

WE HAVE TO KEEP IT SAFE FROM MONSTERS!

IT IS OUR <u>DUTY</u> AS BRAVE KNIGHTS!

WHAT'S <u>THAT</u>?

RUSTLE

AFTER A BUSY DAY IT IS TIME FOR BED

GOOD NIGHT, BUTTER-SCOTCH.

MOM, I'M HOME.

DID YOU HAVE A GOOD DAY PLAYING, SWEETIE?

I HAD SO MANY EPIC ADVENTURES. THERE WERE MONSTERS AND CAVES AND HIDDEN TREASURE!